Shine Bright Kids™
Choose Right. Shine Bright.

Whatever Wanda!

Written by
Christy Ziglar

Illustrated by
Paige Billin-Frye

ideals children's books®
Nashville, Tennessee

ISBN-13: 978-0-8249-5668-4

Published by Ideals Children's Books
A division of Worthy Media, Inc.
Nashville, Tennessee
www.idealsbooks.com

The mark SHINE BRIGHT KIDS and its associated logos
are trademarks of Shine Bright Kid Company, LLC.

Library of Congress Cataloging-in-Publication Data

Ziglar, Christy.
  Whatever Wanda / written by Christy Ziglar ; illustrated by Paige Billin-Frye.
    pages cm — (Shine bright kids)
  Summary: "Wanda learns an important lesson in having a good attitude
when she refuses to cooperate and join in the fun at the Duck Days Festi-
val"— Provided by publisher.
  ISBN 978-0-8249-5668-4 (hardcover : alk. paper) [1. Cooperativeness—
Fiction. 2. Attitude (Psychology)—Fiction. 3. Festivals—Fiction. 4. Conduct
of life—Fiction.] I. Billin-Frye, Paige, illustrator. II. Title.
  PZ7.Z524Wh 2015
  [E]—dc23

                    2014027415

Designed by Georgina Chidlow-Rucker
Printed and bound in China
Leo_Jan15_1

For Mom and Dad: Thank you for
a lifetime of laughter, encouragement,
and family adventures, and for
teaching us where true joy comes
from! And for Jon, Wes, and Ellie:
you make everything more fun!
                              —CZ

DEAR GROWNUPS,

Our attitude impacts everything that we do. How
do we teach our children the importance of staying
positive? It can be challenging to combat the bad
news, examples of poor behavior, and sarcasm
prevalent in our modern culture; yet a positive
attitude is essential for shining bright!

   How do our children see us responding to
disappointment? Do we become frustrated and
negative or do we keep a positive outlook and
remain flexible? Do they see us actively supporting
and engaging in activities and relationships? How
often are we critical without taking action or
offering to help?

   Whether it's learning something new, facing a
difficult situation, or simply getting through the
day, we always have the choice to look on the bright
side. Let's teach our kids that a positive attitude
makes everything better, not to mention a whole
lot more fun! Optimism is contagious and definitely
worth catching.

   Visit www.ShineBrightKids.com for more
parenting resources, games, fun activities, and
worksheets to help your family choose right and
shine bright!

Christy Ziglar

If a frown has found your face,
put a smile in its place.
Change your mind and start to care—
you'll see fun is everywhere!

STAR SEARCH!

Find the star that follows Wanda!
Can you tell whether it is excited or sad?
When Wanda displays a positive attitude,
the star looks happy and bright. When
Wanda's attitude is poor, the star looks
dim and deflated. On each page, notice
the star's mood and try to guess
why it might feel that way.

"We all need a daily checkup
from the neck up to avoid stinkin'
thinkin', which ultimately leads to
hardening of the attitudes."

—ZIG ZIGLAR

"Wanda, time to wake up and get dressed. You don't want to miss the start of the Duck Dash!" her mom called.

The annual Rubber Duck Days festival was the biggest celebration of the year. Everyone looked forward to it. Everyone, that is, but Wanda. She did not understand why an entire town went so crazy over a bunch of ducks.

She pulled the covers back over her head and said,

"WHATEVER!"

"Hurry, now. We want to be on time," her mother called again.

Wanda looked at the clothes on the chair. Her mother had picked out **matching** duck outfits for the whole family.

Wanda did not want to wear any duck outfit, especially not one that matched the rest of her family. She slowly slid off the bed and said,

"WHATEVER."

"Don't you two look adorable?" her mother commented as Wanda joined her brother, Ty, at the breakfast table.

"Do we have to wear these?" Wanda grumbled.

"It's a family tradition," said her mother.

"Wanda, are you excited about the festival?" asked Ty.

She was not. Wanda rolled her eyes and said,

"WHATEVER."

As they reached the Duck Dash starting line, they ran into some friends from school.

Marvin was pulling a wagon. He asked Wanda, "Do you want to run with us? We're handing these out as we go."

That seemed like a lot of extra work to Wanda. She looked down and said,

"WHATEVER."

So her friends ran ahead without her.

The next event was the Duck Derby. Each person chose a rubber duck. All of the ducks were lined up along the edge of the pond and would be pushed off to float to the finish line.

"Would you like to choose your own?" asked the man beside the tub. "This one looks like a winner."

They all looked the same to Wanda. She grabbed the closest duck and said,

"WHATEVER."

Wanda's duck was not a winner— not even close.

Next came the Waddle Walk relay. The team that finished first would get to ride on the main float of the Lucky Duck Parade that afternoon.

Kids lined up to divide into teams and practiced walking in their duck feet.

Marvin went first and picked Willow for his team. Oscar went next and picked Lanie.

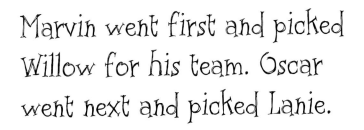

Willow asked, "Wanda, do you want to be on our team?"

Wanda thought the whole thing was silly. She said,

"WHATEVER."

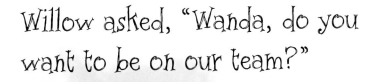

So Willow chose someone else, while Wanda just watched. Everyone seemed to be having so much fun. Wanda just did not get it.

Marvin and Willow's team won!

"Great job, everyone!" said Marvin.

"Good teamwork!" said Willow.

Wanda's father smiled and said,
"Maybe next year, kid."

She thought to herself, *I doubt it.*

Wanda shrugged and said, "WHATEVER."

It was time for the Lucky Duck Parade! Willow and Marvin's team would be riding up front with Waddles, the grand marshall. People started heading to the town square to get ready.

Everyone had a job to do. Wanda's mom was helping with snacks. Her dad was blowing up duck balloons. Ty was his assistant.

The woman in charge asked Wanda what she would like to do. Wanda said, "WHATEVER."

So she was assigned a job that *no one else wanted.*

The winners of the Waddle Walk passed by with some other friends from school. They were on their way to the float for the start of the parade. They waved at Wanda.

Wanda waved back and tried to fake a smile. She said quietly,

"Whatever."

Just then, Waddles was passing by on the other side of the street. She called to Wanda, "Do you want to join your friends?"

"The float is only for the winners," replied Wanda. "I didn't play," she said sadly. "I didn't think it would be fun."

Waddles said gently, "It seems to me that you just need an attitude adjustment. Sometimes you have to believe something *WILL* be great before it actually *IS*.

"Being positive is a choice that makes everything better—not to mention, **a whole lot more fun!**"

Wanda thought about how happy everyone else seemed to be. Then she thought about the way she had been acting. She was the only one not having fun.

"There *IS* one job left. Would you be willing to help?" Waddles smiled and reached out a wing.

Wanda decided it was time to change her mind about ducks.

"I think that sounds like . . ." Wanda paused, then she smiled and said, "FUN!"

"Well, let's go, or we'll miss the parade," said Waddles. Wanda scooped up the last pile of trash and hurried to join her.

Waddles gave Wanda the **perfect job** and the **perfect spot!** She was an instant hit and had the **most fun of all!**

"Who's looking forward to next year's festival?" Waddles asked.

"I am!" yelled Wanda as she gave another "QUACK" out to the crowd. She was POSITIVE it was going to be great!